The SEVEN ½ SINS of STACEY KENDALL

The SEVEN ½ SINS of STACEY KENDALL

by Nancy J. Hopper

A YEARLING BOOK

Published by
Dell Publishing Co., Inc.
1 Dag Hammarskjold Plaza
New York, New York 10017

Yearling ® TM 913705, Dell Publishing Co., Inc.

ISBN: 0-440-47736-0

Reprinted by arrangement with E. P. Dutton, Inc.

Printed in the United States of America

First Yearling printing—December 1983

CW

to Jennifer
because I wrote it for her

1

I often think of life in Miss Jordan's sixth grade as a sort of race. Some days it's a couple of runners bent on breaking four-minute miles. Other times it is two trains on parallel tracks. Occasionally it is just me, Stacey Kendall, against Miss Jordan, trying not to get left behind. I have never had a day in the sixth grade that crawled like a snail.

Today it seemed that we had barely finished discussing a poem and opening our math books when Miss Jordan glanced at her watch and said, "Break time." She gathered her books and papers.

Break time is at eleven o'clock. Mr. Meeker, our principal, has eliminated recess for the sixth grade as he claims we don't need it; but Miss Jordan says even if we don't need it, she does. She gives us exactly fifteen minutes to talk, play games, go to the lavatory, whatever.

"Don't act like a barbarian horde," she ordered us as she swept out of the room. She would return in fifteen minutes with ten times as much energy, two dozen photocopies about new discoveries in science, and at least one new idea.

I lifted my desk lid and pulled out a book covered in plain brown paper. I had written *The Life of the Seal* across the top in big red letters. The actual name of the book is *1,001 Ways To Be Beautiful.* The cover is only to fool my mother, who thinks I should have better things on my mind than my appearance. Personally, I think she is jealous. I mean I might have plain ordinary brown eyes and brown hair and a figure with all the grace and charm of an ironing board, but I do have my youth.

"What's the beauty hint for today?" asked Sharon Meleasson, leaning over me and breathing heavily. I think she breathes that way because she is fat. If she would only lose fifty pounds, she would breathe like everyone else. That's the difference between fat breath and thin breath.

"Give me a minute!" But I wasn't irritated. Just because I was the lucky girl to get the book out of the Media Center first, I was always mobbed by girls on break. It is the only time in my life I have been popular, and I am savoring the experience to remember in my old age.

"I hope it's not dumb like the one on Friday," said Sly Marini, who is known to her parents as Sylvia. "Eat lots of fruit. Geez. That sounds like my mother."

"It means fruit instead of candy and pizza," said Troylene Patterson. She is super at figuring things out.

"Move, Sharon." Sly gave Sharon a shove.

Sharon's piggy little eyes filled with tears, but we all ignored them, including Sharon. It is a price one has to pay for being in the sixth grade and fat.

" 'Splash on a little toilet water every day,' " I read. " 'Put it behind your ears and on your wrists.' "

There was silence except for Sharon's loud breathing. Beyond my little circle, I could hear Tucker Fields and Pete Parsons passing a foam football and yelling, sounding like a barbarian horde.

"Why would anyone want to splash water from the toilet on themselves?" asked Sharon, shock making her voice more whispery than usual. "That isn't even sanitary."

Only Sharon would be ignorant enough not to know what toilet water was. And only Sharon would be foolish enough to admit it.

I had a vision of myself, leaning over the toilet bowl and splashing myself liberally. For a second I felt like throwing up, and then it struck me as funny. "It might be one of the secrets of the stars," I said, giggling. "Why don't you try it, Sharon? You too can be beautiful."

"It would melt that flab right off you," said Sly Marini. "I know—" Her turquoise eyes narrowed like

3

a cat's. "Let's take Sharon down to the lavatory right now and splash her all over with toilet water. We can see if it makes her beautiful."

Sharon took a step backward, a bewildered but wary look on her round face.

"What was yesterday's beauty hint?" asked Jill Williams, as if she needed it.

I glanced up to meet her wide eyes. They are brown like mine, only prettier. Her blonde brown hair is curly and her teeth are perfect. One of the reasons I am reading the book is to find out how to be subtly beautiful like Jill Williams. I want it to happen by the time I am twelve. I have less than one week.

"'Take a bath every day,'" I read, looking back at the book to locate Sunday's hint.

"Every day? Why every day?" asked Sharon.

"To wash off the toilet water," said Troylene.

The football game was getting more active. Tucker scored a goal on the other side of Miss Jordan's desk.

"I wonder if my parents would let me have a nose job for my twelfth birthday," I said. Of course they wouldn't, but I can dream. My mother says I have a classical bridge on my nose. I think it sticks up like a big lump. Everyone knows the bridge of a nose should be indented near the eyes.

"They could lower the bridge and pinch the nostrils," I said, "sort of like Jill's."

"Plastic surgery costs a lot of money," said Troylene.

"Why don't you put a clothespin on it," suggested

4

Sly. "If my nose looked like yours, I'd do anything to improve it."

"I tried that last summer. All I got was two red marks," I muttered. I hadn't realized my nose was that bad. I touched it gently with one finger.

"People," interrupted Miss Jordan, not raising her voice. "People, I had the most exciting idea while I was out on break."

Everyone ran for their seats and grabbed their notebooks before she could get ahead of us.

It's sort of funny. The first week in the sixth grade nobody wanted to try to keep up with Miss Jordan. But by the end of the first month, even Tucker was mad when she was sick and missed a day. He got into two fights and was benched for a week in flag football. He said it was all the substitute's fault. If she had kept him busy the way Miss Jordan did, he wouldn't have had time to get into fights and be benched. Then his team wouldn't have lost two games, either.

"It's a poem on beauty for you to interpret," Miss Jordan said, as if she had just this minute discovered a moped in her Christmas stocking. "'Pied Beauty' by Gerard Manley Hopkins."

The poem was pretty good. As a matter of fact, I like most of the poems she reads to us. Once she read us a long one called *The Lady of Shalott*. I borrowed the book and took it home and read the poem out loud to myself three times.

For weeks I daydreamed about being the lily maid of Astolat. I must have lain in my little boat with my blood slowly freezing a thousand times, my long fair hair trailing in the dark water and the leaves falling upon my dead-pale face. That was real glamour, real elegance.

The door of our room slammed open, punctuating the end of "Pied Beauty." We all knew who was responsible before he strode into the room. Mr. Meeker, our principal, is the only person in the school who enters a classroom without knocking.

"Ah, Miss Jordan," he said, rubbing his hands together and smiling so hard his cheeks looked as if they hurt. "I'm glad to find you in."

Miss Jordan raised one eyebrow. It is a talent of hers.

"Not that I'd expect you anywhere else on a Monday morning." He laughed at his own joke.

We all stared silently.

"Ahem." He cleared his throat. "I have an announcement to make," he said formally, going from his "friendly principal" role to his usual pose. "Mrs. Klein from the Cosmopolitan Club just called me. They have finally arrived at a decision on the winner of the essay contest, Service to Others."

"Big deal," said Tucker. Mr. Meeker didn't notice.

I leaned forward, my attention riveted on Mr. Meeker. I really wanted that award, and I figured I had a good chance. After all, Troylene had been out of town most of the week, at a special class for gifted students. She couldn't possibly have spent all the hours on her essay that I spent on mine.

"The winner," said Mr. Meeker dramatically, "is Stacey Kendall!"

A sound like a sigh swept across the room. I sat back in my seat, suddenly limp. Mother would love this.

"I've already called your parents to give them the good news," said Mr. Meeker, as if reading my thoughts. "I know your mother is pleased that you are following in her footsteps."

For a moment I didn't know what he was talking about. Then I realized he was referring to the fact that Mother works part-time as a writer for the newspaper. Mr. Meeker would think that writing an essay on Service to Others and writing a finance column for *The Review* are one and the same.

"Congratulations, Stacey," said Miss Jordan.

Mr. Meeker frowned. He didn't like attention being taken away from him.

"And the second-place winner," he continued, interrupting the sudden rush of clapping and whistles that filled the room, "is another of Miss Jordan's fine students, Miss Jill Williams!"

Jill turned absolutely pale. She was a natural to score on Service to Others since she is the only person I know who thinks more about other people than she does about herself. She is also terrified of any sort of public attention.

I tore my eyes away from Jill. Mr. Meeker was still speaking.

". . . will read your essay aloud to the student body

in our special awards assembly, Stacey. I can't tell you what an honor that is."

It was an honor. It was the biggest honor I had received in my whole life, and I had earned it entirely by myself. Still, as Mr. Meeker left the room and Miss Jordan went back to talking about poetry, I had a small nagging feeling of dissatisfaction deep inside me. I tried to shove the dissatisfaction away, but I couldn't. Winning the award was great, but nothing was more important to me at almost age twelve than beauty.

2

I have never told my mother about *The Lady of Shalott*. I have never told her about any of the poems that Miss Jordan had us interpret. I'm not so certain she would approve of them. She might think they are sexist or something.

My mother is a really great person, but she is a women's lib type. She is only interested in brains in women. She says beauty is skin-deep, maybe because she isn't exactly beautiful. As a matter of fact, she is sort of plain-looking like me, with brown eyes and short straight brown hair.

That Monday I was really excited, but it wasn't because Miss Jordan had given us a poem about beauty.

It was because Jill Williams had lent me a magazine she had borrowed from her mother. The magazine was all about fashion and makeup and hairstyling. I slammed into the house screaming "I'm home," dropped my books on the coffee table, threw my jacket in the general direction of the closet, and ran upstairs to my room.

Safe inside, I leaned against the door and listened. Either Mother was out somewhere, or she had decided not to pursue me. I sat cross-legged on the floor at the foot of my bed and stared at the cover of the magazine.

There were four women, all of whom had been enormously ugly and whose lives and appearances had been saved by the right hairstyle and the proper makeup. I flipped to the table of contents, where there were loads of exciting articles such as "Women's Ten Best Features," "Your Figure and You," "Daily Diet Discipline," and more. If Mom had caught me with the magazine, she would have grounded me for a week. She only reads *Newsweek* and *Saturday Review.*

The most interesting part of the whole magazine was the advertisements in the back. I turned directly to one which had caught my eye in school.

The full-page ad featured a series of before and after pictures of a woman who had hardly any bust at all in the before picture. In the after picture, her posture was enormously improved, she was smiling, and she had a beautiful figure.

In big black letters, the ad announced:

BUST-TER SIZER!
YOU TOO CAN HAVE
A BEAUTIFUL FIGURE!

I studied the picture. I didn't exactly want a bust that big. People would stop in the street and stare.

I read on. The article promised great improvement in only six weeks. Maybe I could use it for three weeks and have just enough improvement.

The only problem was that the Bust-ter Sizer cost $14.99. I had 35¢. I could hardly borrow the money from Mom. I get only a dollar a week allowance and no advances. Once I saved for a whole month to buy a decent lip gloss, and then Mom wouldn't let me wear it.

Maybe I didn't need the Bust-ter Sizer. It must have been at least three days since I'd checked my figure for improvement. I stripped, then forced myself to stand in front of my mirror and open my eyes.

Until two weeks ago, Miss Jordan used to have a Painting of the Week. She brought in a color reproduction every Tuesday for us to write a paragraph on. A lot of the paintings had fat women in them, some with hardly any clothes on.

Tucker asked why the women were fat, and Miss Jordan explained that the artists liked to paint those large lovely curves and ovals and folds. I stared into my mirror and I knew that none of those artists would ever have wanted to paint me.

11

I didn't have a single curve. The closest I could come were the two lumps at my knees. My bust was nonexistent. As a matter of fact, I was cold at the moment, and some of my goose bumps were larger than my breasts.

I dressed slowly and exercised until dinnertime, all the while plotting how I could get money to buy the Bust-ter Sizer.

When I went downstairs, my dad and my brother, Donovan, who is fourteen, were sitting at the table. Mom was serving the last two plates of spaghetti. She put a plate of spaghetti in front of me and sat down too. Then she said, "Congratulations, Stacey. I'm so proud of you."

"The best essay in the sixth grade," said Dad. "That's great."

"Thank you," I said modestly and lowered my eyes to my plate.

Between shoveling in forkfuls of spaghetti, Donovan started complaining. He always complains. He complains about his teachers and his grades and about cafeteria lunches. Most of all, he complains about his height. He is pretty tall for his age, a whole head taller than I am, but he thinks he is short.

Usually Dad listens to all this and then says something to make Donovan feel better. Or he tries to make a joke, like saying, "You'll just have to take a chair to stand on to kiss the girls good-night." Tonight he was in what he calls his logical mood. When he's in his logical mood, he says a person should analyze everything and then accept it.

12

"I'm sorry, son," he said, "but I think you'd better choose another career besides basketball. Maybe you could get a job stocking the lower shelves in a grocery store."

Donovan's ears turned bright red to match his pimples. "I don't think that's very funny," he said stiffly.

I giggled and choked when a piece of spaghetti went down the wrong pipe.

"It's time to face reality. I'm short, your mother is short, and you are going to be short. We manage to live with it; you can too."

"Isn't there anyone tall in our family?" asked Donovan. He was beginning to sound angry.

"Not that I remember. That's heredity, and heredity is going to determine how tall you are and how wide, the same as it determined that you have brown hair and brown eyes like the rest of us."

"I don't want to be short!" Donovan's howl of anguish and what followed were lost on me. I had my own problems. I slid my eyes sideways to look at Mother.

She was sitting there calmly eating her spaghetti, her long slender hands graceful and pretty. Her hands were the most attractive thing about her, except her hair, which covered her head in a smooth cap. Her features were even, but not spectacular. I studied her figure. She is built a lot like my brother.

There was some hope. My Grandmother Dawson has a figure like Mom's, but I couldn't remember my dad's parents. They had both died in a car crash when I was two.

"What was your mother like?" I blurted, looking at my dad.

He was surprised, but he recovered fast. "She was intelligent and humorous," he said. "Sometimes she had a mean temper, but she never held grudges. She loved animals. When I was a kid, I had two dogs and three cats, a gerbil—"

"I know," I interrupted. I had heard about his animals a thousand times. If I gave him a chance, he'd tell me all their names and what they looked like, even how old they were when they died, and how he buried Rolf under the lilac and Paddy Paws by the garage. Personally, I have only ever had one cat, Stanley, and Stanley was hit by a car last fall.

"What did she look like?" I asked.

Mother rolled her eyes toward the ceiling, but I ignored her. She thinks my interest in beauty is an obsession. I think her interest in grades and scholarship is an obsession.

"Well, she was 5 feet tall, and she had red hair and brown eyes. She weighed about 170. She was a regular beach ball," he said. "But a very nice lady of course," he added quickly.

"So you can take your pick," said Mom. "You can be short and flat like me or short and round like your Grandmother Kendall."

Some pick. I thought I was going to throw up, right on my spaghetti. The only chance I had for a beautiful figure was to stay skinny and to buy the Bust-ter Sizer. At a dollar a week it would take fifteen weeks, and that was without a single candy bar or movie.

"Did Mr. Meeker say when the awards assembly would be?" asked Dad, trying to change the subject. He is a great one for trying to cheer people up.

"I don't know." I was miserable. The fact I had written the best essay in the sixth grade on Service to Others and got to read it aloud in assembly didn't mean a thing to me now. Neither did the fact that I had won a savings bond. My mother would make me keep it forever for my education.

"You should be proud," said Mom. "That is quite an honor."

Honor, I can do without, I reflected gloomily. What I needed was money.

3

If I really wanted to, I could blame all my present problems on Jill Williams. After all, she is the person who began the series of events that almost led to my being kicked out of the Medford School. But then, blaming Jill wouldn't really be honest. I suppose it would be a lot like Tucker's blaming the substitute teacher for his getting into fights. Miss Jordan says always to tell the truth; that way you don't have to remember what you said.

Well, the truth is that I am somewhat jealous of Jill Williams. Somewhat. The real truth is that I am green with envy, knock-down-and-drag-out seething with jealousy of Jill Williams. How can anyone be so pretty and be nice too? Life just isn't fair.

Tuesday, Jill came to school with her ears pierced. She had the prettiest little gold studs in them, shaped like daisies. They made her look elegant, and Jill doesn't need any beauty aids.

Of course we all gathered around Jill during break, all the girls that is. The boys were talking about stupid macho things, like next year's Super Bowl.

"It didn't hurt at all," Jill insisted, after Sly Marini asked her for the fortieth time. "I hardly felt it. The lady put something cold on my ears first to make them numb."

"An ice cube?" I asked.

"Of course not, dummy," said Sly. "An ice cube would have melted all over her top."

"It felt like an ice cube," said Jill.

"I begged and begged Mom to let me get my ears pierced," said Sharon, "and she wouldn't let me."

"My mom would," I said. The words popped out before I could think. That was okay. Technically it wasn't the truth, but it wasn't the kind of lie that could cause trouble.

"For sure," said Sly in that ugly, sneering tone she uses when she is jealous. She and Jill have this sort of running competition for the class beauty queen. I don't think Jill is aware of the contest, but with two little holes in her ears she had surged way out in front of Sly.

"She would," I said stubbornly. And then to my absolute horror I heard myself say, "As a matter of fact, I am getting my ears pierced for my twelfth birthday, which is Sunday."

In the silence that followed, I prayed that that had not been my voice saying those words, but I knew it was. The other girls were staring at me, disbelief on their faces. Sharon had a silly grin all over her round face.

"I might even get it done tonight," I blurted to fill the silence. It wasn't exactly a lie. If I wished so completely for it to happen, it might. At least I told myself that.

"I'll believe it when I see it," said Sly.

"I'm going to get my ears pierced for sure," said Troylene. She didn't sound convinced.

"If Stacey can get it done, anyone can," said Sly.

"What do you mean by that?" I was starting to get mad. Where was Miss Jordan? We were supposed to be studying the monsoon season in the Far East. Why wasn't she here, making us do our work?

"Everyone knows what your mother is like."

"What is she like?" If Sly said one single solitary thing about my mother, I was going to punch her right in the nose. I might complain about Mom, but that's my privilege, not Sly's.

"She—"

"Hey, did you work on that poem yet?" Jill interrupted.

Sly stopped glaring at me long enough to glare at her. Jill was the real target of her hostility anyway.

"I have better things to do than to think about a stupid old poem," she said.

"I have two paragraphs written already," said Troylene. That is typical of Troylene. She almost always has an A interpretation.

I was so relieved at Jill's breaking up the argument with Sly, that I let my mouth take charge again. "I wish we could do *The Lady of Shalott* again," I said. "I loved it."

"So did I," said Troylene. "I wrote five pages on it."

"For weeks I dreamed I was lying in a little boat," I said, "my fair hair trailing in the water."

"Your hair isn't fair," said Sly.

"Well, it's fairer than yours," I snapped. Her hair is long and black, silky shiny.

"I dreamed about that too," breathed Sharon, "drifting along with the leaves falling on my face."

We all stared at her.

"My God," said Sly. "Can't you just see it? She'd swamp the boat."

Even Jill laughed. I tried not to, but the thought of Sharon all squinched up in a little boat, weighing it down with her flab so that the waves swept over the sides and soaked her, was too much. I started to giggle and before I knew it, I was laughing right out loud. By that time Sly was bent over double, tears coming as she gasped for air, pointing at Sharon.

At that moment Miss Jordan came back. I didn't have time to laugh at Sharon or to think of what terrible trouble my mouth had gotten me into until four when school let out.

Then I thought about it a lot. I thought positively, which is what my dad is always telling me to do. He says positive thinking has a lot to do with a person's success in life. Evidently, it doesn't have much to do with convincing your mother to let you get your ears pierced.

I tried to lead into it gradually. I eased up beside her at the kitchen counter and grabbed a piece of carrot which she was chopping for salad.

Mother swatted at my fingers with her chopping knife. Some day she is going to really let me have it, and then we are both going to be sorry.

"I decided what I want for my birthday," I said.

"Today's decision on the gift," said Mom, grinning at me.

"This time I'm serious." She was referring to the fact that every other day I have a new idea of what I want. What I really wanted was a twenty-dollar bill, but Mom says that giving money as a present is tacky.

"What?" she asked, looking directly at me.

I took a deep breath. "Jill Williams got her ears pierced," I said.

"She has holes in her ears?" Mom made it sound as if Jill had a bone in her nose, maybe the thigh bone of a zebra.

"She looks great."

"I didn't think the Williamses were that kind of people."

"What kind?"

"The kind that would permit their daughter to mutilate her body."

Somehow, I didn't think that Mom was going to let me get my ears pierced.

"I hope you never do that," she said, fixing me with her gimlet eyes. *Gimlet* was a word I learned in Miss Jordan's class. It means a small tool for boring holes, in other words, Mom's eyes at the moment.

"Of course not," I said agreeably. My life was ruined.

"Because I wouldn't want you to do that," she said.

"I figured that out." I backed away and beat a retreat to my room where I stood and stared in the mirror, willing myself to change.

I didn't change one little bit; but while I stood there, I had an idea. Mom hadn't exactly forbidden me to get my ears pierced. She had only said she hoped I would never do that. I licked my lips and looked closer, into my eyes.

I could have pierced ears, and it wouldn't cost me one single cent.

4

The trouble with our house is there is never any privacy. There isn't even any privacy for your thoughts, let alone your actions.

"The Williamses' daughter had holes put through her ears," Mother announced at the dinner table.

"Was it an accident or did it happen on purpose?" asked my dad.

"Ellen Rivers has pierced ears. She wears these tiny gold hoops," Donovan said in a dreamy voice. Then he turned bright red.

"I think it's obscene," said my mother. "I can't imagine what her parents must have in their heads, permitting her to do a thing like that."

"We'd never want to do anything like that, would we?" said Dad. Then he winked at me.

Fortunately, Mom didn't notice. She was digging a hole for gravy in her mashed potatoes. She is the only adult female I know who does that.

After she finished the hole, she filled it, all the while talking about foolish children with irresponsible parents. All of a sudden she stopped talking and stared at Donovan. After a second she demanded, "Who is Ellen Rivers and what is she doing with holes in her ears?"

While Donovan turned redder and Mom kept asking him questions about Ellen Rivers, I ate my pork chops and peas and salad. I didn't eat any gravy or mashed potatoes because *1,001 Ways To Be Beautiful* says starches and gravies are very dangerous for the figure, especially the trouble spots. Normally I would have joined in teasing Donovan, but I had my mind on other things. I was only filling in time as well as my stomach. I tried to think of it as preparing myself physically and emotionally for the evening's event.

I helped Mom do the dishes. Then I filled a glass with ice cubes and went into the bathroom.

As I said, there is no privacy anywhere in our house. No sooner had I laid out all my implements in a neat arrangement and fitted an ice cube into my washcloth than Donovan was pounding on the door.

"I want in there," he yelled.

I tried to ignore him.

"Stacey, you get out of there. Mom! Mom! Stacey's hogging the bathroom."

"Stacey," Mom called from the kitchen. "You hurry now."

"I can't wait!" yelled Donovan.

"Why is there always a line when I want in the john?" said my father.

That was too much. I gathered my equipment together and moved my home surgery to my bedroom.

There I laid it all out in a neat row on my dresser top. The light wasn't very good because I keep it very dim, so I can't see my complexion. I took the lamp off my desk and plugged it in next to my dresser. Then I eyed my equipment.

There was a bar of soap, a thick needle for sewing on coat buttons, a black permanent marker, one of those pushpins for bulletin boards, and two straight pins bent in half. I also had my glass of ice cubes and my washcloth.

I leaned forward and looked into the mirror. My complexion looked pretty good, even under the additional light. Evidently my sacrifice of foods I liked was paying off. My hair was clean, and if I squinted a little, I could imagine highlights.

I picked up the needle and looked at it. It looked positively vicious. Besides, it would be difficult to push in and to keep straight at the same time. I laid it to one side, along with the permanent marker. Then I picked up the pushpin. I tested the point against my index finger and measured to be certain that it would go the whole way through my lobe. Next I stuck it into the bar of soap to sterilize it.

I was ready. Folding an ice cube carefully into my washcloth, I held it behind the lobe of my right ear, all the while staring at myself solemnly in the mirror. My eyes were very big with a greenish tinge to them. Upon close inspection, I discovered that this was a result of the pupils' reflecting the green walls of my room. The pupils reflected because they were very large, the way my cat Stanley's eyes used to get when he was frightened.

Resting my elbows on the dresser and staring intently at my earlobe, I took the pin in my right hand.

A scratch and a pop and the pin went through.

There was hardly any blood at all. What there was, I wiped away carefully before I inserted the first straight pin. Then I observed the results.

The tiny head of the straight pin looked almost like the silver head of an ear stud. The bent part hardly showed at all. I moved my head. It swung gently.

The second ear was a breeze. I even cut down on my ice-cube time and it didn't hurt at all. Well, only a little. I told myself that my eyes were red from the strain.

When I had finished, I had a strange feeling in my stomach. It was a mixture of sweet success and fear over what Mom might do when she found out. I took my brush and brushed my hair carefully over my ears to hide the pins. Then I brushed it up again so I could stare at myself.

Pierced ears were a definite improvement. Even with the pins for earrings I looked a lot older, a lot more mysterious.

Now if I only had the money for the Bust-ter Sizer. Somehow, someway, I had to get the money.

I looked in the mirror, and I had this really great idea. At least it seemed like a great idea at the time.

5

Ear-piercing Clinic
Thursday morning break $1.00
Girls' lavatory near the Media Center
Silvery Studs   One day only
Pass it on

I had a stroke of good luck. Right before morning
break on Wednesday, Mrs. Withers came to the door.
Mrs. Withers teaches one of the other three sections
of sixth grade. I am using the word *teaches* loosely.
What she does is have them make drawings and do
work sheets while she paints her nails and eats candy.

27

Every time one of the parents complains and Mr. Meeker calls her for a discussion, Mrs. Withers comes whining to Miss Jordan. Miss Jordan unloads some of her great ideas on Mrs. Withers, and for a few days her students learn things. Then it's back to the work sheets and the fingernail painting.

There had been three parents in the day before. Mrs. Withers whispered and whined while I passed my note around the class, to girls only. From behind the cover of my science book, I watched the teachers at the front of the room.

Mrs. Withers is short and blonde and sort of pretty except that she has a weak, sulky mouth. She is nice until she doesn't get her own way, and then she can be very mean. Right now she looked as if she hadn't gotten her own way much lately.

Miss Jordan was listening to her, but her eyes kept straying toward the classroom and her mouth was tight at the corners, the way it gets when she is disgusted. Mostly her mouth gets tight around Mrs. Withers, but it also happened Tuesday two weeks ago, when Mr. Meeker took away her art reproductions of half-naked fat women and locked them in the school safe. One of the parents had complained that his son was being exposed to pornography. Miss Jordan explained that his son was being exposed to great art, but the parent didn't care at all. He said great art doesn't belong in the elementary school.

Right now Miss Jordan's mouth was almost as tight as it was that Tuesday. Finally she announced break five minutes early and left the room with Mrs. Withers. Immediately, Tucker ran to the door and stuck his head out to listen.

"Alethea's giving her hell," he shouted. Alethea is Miss Jordan's first name. It means truth.

Tucker said something else, but I couldn't hear it. My desk was completely surrounded by girls, and for once they weren't looking for my book on beauty.

"Who's going to pierce ears?" demanded Bonnie Adriani. She is the most developed girl in the sixth grade. The boys call her Body Adriani.

"I am," I said.

There was a silence while the girls thought about that.

At last Troylene asked, "How do we know you can pierce ears?"

Casually I flipped my hair back. This was the moment I had been waiting for.

"Wow," said Sharon.

"You did that?" asked Sly.

"Myself."

"Let me see." Sharon reached forward.

"Don't touch!"

"Are they sore?"

"No." I didn't want her fat germy fingers all over my ears.

"Then why can't I touch?"

"Because I don't want you to."

She looked sulky. "I think a dollar's too much," she said, sliding her eyes sidewise.

"You'd think ten cents was too much," said Sly. She was definitely interested.

"My clinic is Thursday break only," I announced. "And keep it quiet. If the boys find out they'll tell, and then none of you will have your ears pierced."

Sly was staring at my earlobes. "Did it hurt?"

"Not one bit."

"Why are you wearing straight pins in your ears?"

"It's the new style." I looked her straight in the eyes. "In Sweden all the women are wearing straight pins in their ears."

"All of them?"

"All but one or two dumpy old hags."

The girls looked doubtful. I figured that my clinic could go either way, boom or bust.

"I'm taking reservations," I said. "I need to know how many of you want to sign up. My time is limited."

"I don't know." Troylene's voice trailed off. I think she was beginning to chicken out.

"I always wanted my ears pierced," said Bonnie, "but I was going to wait and go to Murphy Mart."

"Maybe you can wait," said Sly, "but I'm not going to. I'm going to get my ears pierced tomorrow morning."

I breathed a little easier. Where Sly went, so would the other girls. Sylvia can be very nasty when you don't go along with her ideas.

Sharon was first to agree. "I can always take my earrings off to weigh myself," she said.

"Me too," said Bonnie.

That was only three. The other girls stood around like big lumps. Three dollars wouldn't be enough for the Bust-ter Sizer.

"I know a couple of kids in Mrs. Withers' class who are dying to have their ears pierced," said Sly suddenly. "Missy Sales and maybe Pam."

"Mrs. Withers doesn't give a break," I said. "So that lets them out."

"Mrs. Withers' class is all break," said Sly. "Her students can leave the room whenever they want to. She's glad to get rid of them."

"Okay." Caution gave way to greed. "Tell them to be in the lavatory at eleven."

"What are you going to do, play poker?" asked Pete Parsons. He had sneaked up on us and caught the last sentence.

"None of your business," said Bonnie.

"Says who?" asked Pete.

Bonnie answered him, but he wasn't paying attention. He was only pretending to listen while he stared at her body. At that moment I wasn't certain I wanted the bust-building equipment.

"Where's my note?" I asked, my voice high from tension.

No one knew. I had a tiny feeling that something might go wrong with my great idea. Trying to think positively, I shoved the feeling far out of my mind.

6

"Did anyone find my note?" I asked first thing when I got to school on Thursday.

"No." Sly sounded very cheerful. "Did you bring the stuff?"

"Sure." I had carefully assembled everything the evening before and packed it in my purse. I had equipped myself with two pushpins, one for spare, a bar of soap, some tissues, and ten sets of carefully bent straight pins. I was about to make my fortune.

"Are you nervous?"

"Of course not. What do I have to be nervous about?" I demanded.

"Just checking."

Fortunately Miss Jordan came in at that moment, and the day was off and running. I was glad because I was very nervous. Sweat was running down my sides from my armpits, and my hands felt cold and shaky. Also I had an upset stomach. On the whole, I felt in no shape to perform surgery in the girls' lavatory over break.

I still didn't feel in any shape to do surgery when eleven o'clock rolled around, but by that time Sly was eager for action and I am not in the habit of arguing with her.

"I have to go to the cafeteria to get some ice," I stalled.

"It's coming. I told Missy to pick it up on her way," she said.

"Oh." I leaned weakly against the nearest sink. I knew there would be a lot of girls, but I had never pictured this many. It was hot in the lavatory, and the air smelled used. The room was small and hot and not very clean. I was having difficulty breathing. I hoped I would faint.

"Here you are." Missy charged in with a glass full of cubes.

"Any trouble?"

"No. I said the cubes were for Miss Jordan's class. The lady just rolled her eyes and handed them over."

Praying for a fire drill, I took my equipment out of my purse and arranged it on a paper towel on the shelf over the sink.

"You first." Sly pushed Missy forward.

"No. I don't want to go first."

"Too bad."

Missy was backed up against the sink. Forgetting the ice cubes, I seized the pushpin in my right hand and grabbed an earlobe with my left.

"She has her eyes closed!" shrieked Missy.

"I do not." I opened them.

"Shut up," ordered Sly.

Missy whimpered.

I jabbed. The pin went through the lobe and stuck in my finger. I jerked it free.

"When are you going to do it?" asked Missy.

"It's done," I said, sucking my finger. The second ear I stuffed an ice cube behind. It saved my finger and also numbed Missy's ear. In another two seconds I had inserted my first pair of ear studs.

"One dollar," I said. "From now on everybody pays first." My stomachache was gone and my hands had stopped shaking.

The other girls stared at Missy. She turned to examine herself in the mirror and smiled, moving her head from side to side.

"They're in straight," said Troylene.

"Next," I said professionally.

I operated on Sly next, then on two girls from other rooms that I didn't recognize. I pierced Bonnie's ears and Troylene's. The money piled up. The pile of tissues became bloodier.

"My turn," said Sharon, pushing her way to the front. She stopped, staring at my bent pins.

"Those don't look like silver to me," she said.

"Picky, picky."

"Your note said silver."

"It said *silvery*. What do you want for a dollar, emeralds and rubies?"

"Get out of my way, Sharon." Pam pushed past and handed me a dollar.

"But I want my ears pierced!" howled Sharon.

"Wait your turn." I was getting tired. It seemed I had been punching holes in people for hours. I was wishing I had charged a dollar an ear. I took aim at Pam's ear and missed.

"Stand back," I ordered. "I need air."

I stabbed again.

I guess I could say that Pam was my first failure. The hole in her left ear was definitely lower than the hole in her right ear, and it bled a lot. She turned very white and sat down abruptly on the nearest toilet.

"I feel funny," she said.

"It's your imagination," I said.

"There's blood on my blouse."

"That's okay." I held the last of my cubes to her ear. The blood slowed and dripped.

"What will I tell my mom?" she protested. "This is my best blouse."

"Tell her you had a nosebleed," said Sly.

Pam leaned over and put her head between her knees. When she sat up, there was more color in her cheeks. I breathed a sigh of relief.

"That's all," I announced. "Clinic's closed."

A rumble of discontent mixed with one of relief. Sharon pulled at one of my arms.

"I want my ears pierced," she said.

"Go to Murphy Mart."

"I can't. I only have a dollar." She held out four grubby quarters.

"Clinic's closed," I repeated.

There was a knocking on the lavatory door. "Break's over," screamed Pete Parsons from the other side.

"I'll tell," said Sharon.

"I don't have time."

"Just hurry." She grabbed my arm again.

I dropped the pushpin on the floor and picked it up.

"Do it!" ordered Sly. "I'll watch the hall." She stood by the door as the other girls poured out of the lavatory.

I took the quarters, seized Sharon's left ear and pushed. She gave a little gasp as the pin went through.

"Miss Jordan," hissed Sylvia.

That was it. I shoved a tissue at Sharon while I dumped my equipment into the trash can. By the time Miss Jordan was at the door, I was halfway out.

"What are you girls doing?" she asked.

"Nothing," I mumbled.

"Pam had a nosebleed," said Sly. "We were helping her."

Miss Jordan's calm gray eyes assessed us. She nodded briefly and then turned away.

"Come on. Let's hold our discussions in more pleasant surroundings," she said.

We were lucky. Mrs. Knopf, my fifth grade teacher, would have had the truth out of us in a minute. Mrs. Knopf believes that everyone is up to evil when they aren't, while Miss Jordan is exactly the opposite. She believes even Tucker is innocent until proven guilty.

It was good to go back to room sixteen and to sit at my desk. Compared to the lavatory, the atmosphere was light and airy, the room pleasant and cheerful with its pale yellow walls and green chalkboards. I stretched my legs out under my desk and gave myself over to language arts.

Several times in the next hour I noticed Sharon staring at me from across the room, but it wasn't until one o'clock in the cafeteria that I found out why.

"You only pierced one of my ears," she said.

"I did?" I was honestly amazed. In the confusion, I thought I had done both of them.

"I look ridiculous. You have to do the other one."

"I can't. I threw away the equipment." I almost said the evidence, but I didn't think that would sound very good.

Sharon's face turned red and her eyes folded into the fat creases around them.

"You have to," she insisted. "What am I going to do with one pierced ear?"

"Maybe you could join a motorcycle gang. I heard they only wear one earring," I suggested helpfully.

I fished two quarters out of my purse. "Here. Here's your refund."

The rest of the day Sharon glared at me every time she could catch my eyes. I don't know why she was so mad. I only charged her fifty cents.

7

"Is everything all right?" Mom asked when I came in the door from school.

"Of course." A shiver ran down my spine. She was looking directly at me. Any minute now she would see the pins through my ears.

"You look pale."

"I'm tired. I didn't get my break today. I worked right through it."

Fortunately, she didn't ask at what. At that moment Donovan came in and headed for the kitchen. Mom ran to protect the contents of the refrigerator.

I put my coat and books away and flopped on the couch. I really was tired, tired and very depressed. I had pierced all those ears and been devious with Miss

Jordan; and I only had seven dollars and fifty cents. That wasn't nearly enough for the Bust-ter Sizer. Besides, the more I thought about Body Adriani and the way Pete Parsons stared at her, the less I wanted the Bust-ter Sizer. Maybe I would wait for nature to make me round or flat. I yawned.

I must have fallen asleep, because the next thing I knew Dad was home.

"What's the matter, Stacums?" he asked. "Have a rough day?"

"Don't call me that," I said automatically. I am much too old to have a pet name, but secretly I like it.

"You must be tired." He sat beside me. "To fall asleep like that."

"I guess so." I was only half-awake and still depressed. I sounded like it.

"Tell you what. Suppose tonight I dry the dishes, and you read the paper after dinner," he said. "You can be Mr. Kendall, home from a tough session of executive decisions."

"Oh, Dad," I giggled.

At that moment Mom came into the room, looking brisk. She is always looking brisk. She even looks brisk at seven in the morning, when I am wondering what I am doing out of bed and how I will make it until seven fifteen.

"What's all this about?"

"I worked out a deal with Stacey. Tonight I dry the dishes."

"This is Thursday. Thursday, Donovan washes and Stacey dries."

"So tonight, Donovan washes and George dries."

"You spoil her."

"Yep." He poked a finger into my ribs.

"George, I don't approve of that."

"What's for dinner?" He changed the subject.

"Chicken." Mother looked a little wary, aware that she had been sidetracked. "You spoil her because she's a girl," she said, but her voice had lost its punch. I hurried to help put food on the table.

Dinner went smoothly. For once, Donovan shut up with his complaints. He was probably fantasizing about Ellen Rivers. I was thinking about Troylene and Sly and all the other girls I had pierced during the break, wondering if any one of them would squeal and tell their parents who had done it and if their parents would do anything if they did find out.

My parents were holding what my mom calls adult conversation. That usually means they talk about what they did that day and what happened on the news.

I listened while I stuffed myself. I even ate all of my rice and two pieces of black Russian pumpernickel bread. I was still depressed, and when I am depressed, eating makes me feel better.

"Did you get the programming straightened out?" I heard Mom ask. My dad is some sort of computer programmer, although I don't know what kind.

"Yeah. It turned out that dumb blonde in Kraf-

chak's office fed two wrong spaces into the machine."
His cup made a tiny *clink* against his saucer.

"What *dumb blonde*?" Mother stressed the last two
words, so Dad should have been warned, but he is
very innocent. He never seems aware of traps until he
falls right into them.

"I don't know." He sounded weary. "They all look
alike. Red nails, red lips, fad clothes, nothing in their
heads."

"Oh." Now her voice sounded really tight. "All
dumb blondes look alike. Right?"

At last Dad caught it. He lifted his eyes slowly from
his chicken and rice. "You know what I mean," he
said carefully.

"I know exactly what you mean."

He didn't answer.

"That sounded sexist to me."

"Anne—"

"I don't think that's the kind of thinking Stacey
and Donovan should be exposed to."

"Are you accusing me of something?"

"I am merely stating that you have been so brain-
washed by our society that you make obvious sexist
statements without even being aware of it."

"Anne, she *is* a dumb blonde. If she were a he, then
he would be a dumb blond!" He put down his fork.
His eyes glittered. My dad might seem like a mild-
mannered person, but he doesn't ever let anyone walk
on him.

"That phrase is never, ever used in reference to
men."

"Maybe for a reason."

"George Kendall!"

"Before dinner, you were accusing me of spoiling Stacey because she is a girl. Now you are accusing me of being some sort of monster who looks down on women. You can't have it both ways." His voice gradually gained momentum. I stopped eating.

"Spoiling is a form of sexism."

"Then you are sexist because you permit Donovan to go places and do things that you won't permit Stacey to do," said Dad.

"I didn't do nothing." Donovan looked bewildered. The gradually rising voices had broken into his fantasy life.

"Don't you?" pushed Dad.

"That's because he's older." Mom lost a little of her confidence.

"I suppose you'll let Stacey go bowling by herself when she's fourteen?"

I could have cheered. Mom is always telling me I am too old to do one thing, or else I am too young to do something else. All the time I know it is only an excuse.

"In a bowling alley?" She stalled for time.

"That's where people bowl."

There was a long silence.

"Well?" said Dad.

"That's different," said Mom. She looked at her plate.

"Exactly."

There was another silence. Then Mom looked up.

She glanced at me and then at Donovan and then at my dad.

"That doesn't make it fair," she said, each word quiet but very distinct.

Sometimes I get mad at my mother because she is so different from other girls' mothers. She isn't interested in clothes or hairstyling or gossip. She seems touchy and rigid and far away from me in her ideas. Then she says something that shows that, way down deep at the bottom, she really and truly understands.

At that moment, I could have hugged and kissed her. Instead I sat on my chair and waited for what would happen next.

"I know it isn't fair," said my dad. "I don't like it either, but it is reality. We have to deal with reality and teach Stacey and Donovan to deal with it too."

"I realize that." Mom sounded a little depressed. "I still think you ought to watch what you say."

"I know. I try."

They stared at each other, the food on their plates forgotten. It almost seemed as if I could have put out my hand and touched that stare as it passed between one person and the other.

"I have an idea," said Mom.

"What?"

"Why not tonight have Anne wash and George dry?"

"Super idea." He smiled.

Not all my parents' arguments end like that. Sometimes they go on for days until both Mom and Dad are worn and sullen and even the air in the house seems thick and nasty.

By all accounts I should have been overjoyed. They were at peace; I had very little homework; I didn't have to dry the dishes; and I was seven dollars and fifty cents richer. Instead, as I left the table and went to the living room to watch television, I had a sense of ever-deepening despair.

8

"All hell broke loose" was an expression I had heard but never completely understood until Friday at school. All hell really did break loose. You wouldn't think people would make so much fuss over a few holes.

There was an air of tense excitement in Miss Jordan's room as I entered that morning. Almost everybody was looking at me, and it was plain that kids who hadn't even been near the ear-piercing clinic knew all about it. Even the boys knew. Pete Parsons gave me a look of deep speculation, and Tucker made a sign of power, his tightly clenched fist straight up in the air.

Only Miss Jordan seemed as usual, full of energy and good spirits. She ignored the confusion before the bell, the students milling around aimlessly, swarming at her as she wrote on the chalkboard. I sat in my seat and watched her, trying to detect evidence that she knew I had been playing surgeon the day before.

Because of Miss Jordan's superior slender height, she was easy to see among the crowd of students. I didn't get much of a chance to watch her though. Sly passed by my seat, not stopping to speak, and dropped a note on my desk.

THEY ARE ON TO YOU!
WATCH OUT!
MEEKER IS OUT TO GET YOU!

The note was printed in capital letters and was edged in black. It didn't make me feel one bit better. I looked anxiously at Sly but she was in her seat, and Miss Jordan was collecting our math homework.

Once during the morning, I glanced up to see Missy and Pam peeking into our room, watching me. I guess they wanted to know if I had been suspended yet or not. All I know is the sight of those two staring at me from the hall didn't do a thing for my digestive system. My stomach kept flip-flopping like a fish out of water.

During the break, the girls came to my desk as usual.

"Boy are you in trouble," said Sly. She sounded absolutely overjoyed at the idea.

"Why?"

"Someone found your note and turned it over to the principal. I heard he contacted all the mothers, and they're having a special meeting at the school this afternoon to decide what to do with you."

"Who told?" Rage made my voice thick.

"Not me." Troylene sounded as depressed as I felt. She was pale and her usually smooth milk-chocolate skin was sort of washed-out and ashy looking. I hoped it didn't have anything to do with my messing with her ears.

I did a quick check on the girls around my desk to see which ones were still wearing their silvery studs. Sly was, and Troylene and Bonnie. I looked at Sharon.

Her little eyes looked back with absolutely no expression whatsoever in them. They matched her flat expressionless face. Her right ear was normal. Her left earlobe glowed bright red, like a Christmas tree ball. It was so swollen that it poked out from beneath her yellow hair.

I swallowed. I tried, but I couldn't take my eyes off her ear. I attempted a friendly smile, but I felt as if I were baring my teeth like an animal.

"Sharon had an infection," said Sly. "She'll probably die of blood poisoning."

"I will not."

"Maybe you'll only lose an ear." Sly grinned at her and added generously, "Don't worry. You can wear your hair long. Hardly anyone will notice."

Sharon didn't answer. She was staring at Sly as if

Sly had just crawled out from under a rock. At least she wasn't looking at me.

"Hey," said Jill softly. "It isn't the end of the world."

I fought back tears. For me it was. I wondered if the school would still give me the award for Service to Others. I wondered if they would have stocks built, like in olden times, and put me in them on the playground as an example for the kindergartners. I wondered if it would help me to refund the money I had collected.

I couldn't eat lunch. They had my favorite—french fries and Fritos and batter-dipped fish—but I only sat and looked at the food.

"Aren't you going to eat?" Sharon sat across from me.

I shook my head.

"Don't let it go to waste." She deftly substituted her empty hot tray for my full one.

"No wonder you're fat like a pig," said Sly. "You're a human garbage disposal."

"The fatter I get, the less people will notice my missing ear," said Sharon cheerfully. For the gift of a cafeteria lunch, she had forgiven me.

Mr. Meeker wasn't so understanding. Right after cafeteria, Miss Jordan took me aside and told me I was to report to his office.

"Should I take my books?"

"Why?" She looked startled.

"Maybe I won't be coming back."

Tucker whistled and stamped his feet. Pete made a victory sign. Sly smiled a sleek satisfied smile, and Jill Williams gave me a sympathetic glance.

I reported to the office minus my books. Miss Jordan had more confidence in my survival than I did.

It was a sign of the seriousness of my deed that I wasn't permitted to sit and suffer on the chairs outside his door, while Mr. Meeker debated my fate inside. Instead, he ushered me right into his office.

I had been there before, but on that day it all seemed new to me—the faded brown filing cabinets, the darker brown curtains with ducks flying south on them. There was a little figure of a man with a golf club on the windowsill. I stared at that, trying to act casual.

"No calls," Mr. Meeker told Miss Bell, his secretary. He indicated the chair in front of his desk, and I seated myself. He went around the desk, shuffled a few papers on its broad surface, picked up a neatly folded note, studied it, and looked at me. I looked back, hoping that steady eyes would be a point in my favor.

Every time I see Mr. Meeker, I picture him rubbing his hands together and looking *unctuous*. That is a word Miss Jordan made us learn for what she calls the word for the day. It means oily, but only when applied to people, not to cars and cooking.

Anyway, Mr. Meeker is definitely unctuous. He is small and narrow with blue eyes and thin blond hair which he wears smoothed across the bald spot on the top of his head. His hair is definitely oily, and I don't mean unctuous.

After a few seconds he refolded the note and dropped it back on his desk.

"I take it you know the contents of that note," he said.

I nodded.

"Did you write it?"

I nodded again, not trusting my voice.

"I have been made aware that," he continued in his low voice, "yesterday morning you—um—pierced the ears of some of your classmates in the girls' lavatory." He studied his hands, glanced out the window, then back at me. "The lavatory next to the Media Center," he added, as if that made the crime more ugly.

My head bobbed again. I was beginning to feel like one of those artificial cats or dogs that people put in the back windows of their cars to nod their heads at traffic lights.

"Do you have anything to say for yourself?"

"No," I croaked.

There was another silence while we held a staring contest. He won.

"Do you realize the seriousness of this situation?"

"Yes."

"I tried to contact your mother by telephone to meet us here, but she was unavailable."

A cold sweat started in my armpits and ran down my sides. This was worse than I had imagined.

"Couldn't we let my mother out of this?"

"Hardly. It's a little too late for that." He sighed. "I don't understand, Stacey. You have always been a model student. I don't think I have ever in six years had you in this office for disciplinary purposes."

"There's a first time for everything," I said, trying to inject a light note into our conversation.

He ignored it. "Considering your record," he continued, "we have to think long and carefully about this situation before we take action. I want to be certain I have all the facts, that the facts are correct, and that I hear all sides of the story. Therefore, I am going to have a meeting of all concerned parents Monday morning. I would like you and your mother to attend that meeting."

"Couldn't you just suspend me now?" I suggested weakly.

"Without a hearing?" His blue eyes surveyed me sadly as he shook his head. "I don't think so. For now, I am going to ask that you report here with your mother at ten Monday morning. I have prepared a note for your mother to that effect. You may collect it from Miss Bell on your way out." He hesitated. "I would, ah, suggest that you might like to acquaint your parents with the situation before that meeting."

He sat down abruptly and began working on some of the papers covering his desk. I was dismissed. I left his office and picked up the note from Miss Bell. All the time, the sick feeling inside me was getting sicker.

The worst part of the whole mess was that someone,

some girl I knew, had kept that note of mine to hand in to the office the first chance she got. Someone had planned to inform on me. But who? I thought of Sharon and her red swollen ear. She probably had good cause to be a traitor. But even so, I just couldn't believe Sharon would be that mean.

My mind turned from Sharon. I had bigger worries. Somehow, sometime between now and Monday morning at ten o'clock, I had to tell Mom that I was in the deepest trouble of my life.

9

It was a lot easier for Mr. Meeker to tell me to acquaint my parents with the situation than it was for
me to acquaint them with it. Until I read his note, I
was hoping that he had written the bad news down on
paper, but Mr. Meeker never likes to offend parents.
He had merely requested that one or both of them be
present in his office at ten o'clock on Monday and left
the hard part of telling them up to me.

For one wild moment, I envisioned convincing Dad
to go with me instead of Mother. Then that reality
Dad is always talking about asserted itself. He can
never take time off from work. Since Mom works part-
time as a reporter for *The Review,* her hours are

pretty much her own choice. She always represents both of them at school functions.

Maybe Mother could write up my case as a newspaper story, I thought gloomily. That way, she would forgive me because she got something out of it. My gloom deepened as I remembered that she works mostly on the financial and business pages. Somehow I didn't think my case fit those pages, even with my profit motive.

• I marched into the house, put away my coat and books, and went straight to the kitchen. It didn't help my morale that she was sitting at the table working on income tax forms, but I strengthened my resolve.

"Mom," I said.

"Yes?" She looked up, her eyes glazed from hours of struggling with numbers.

"You remember how you are always telling me to think for myself?"

"Yes." Her eyes cleared a little.

I took a deep breath.

"Stacey, what do you have on your ears?"

My breath wheezed out, like a dying balloon.

"What is that?" She half rose to get a better look.

I could almost follow her thinking in her eyes. It went something like: Stacey has something on her ears. Stacey has something *in* her ears. Oh, no. Stacey has straight pins in her ears.

"You mutilated yourself!" she screamed.

I gasped.

"Oh. I don't believe it." She grasped her cheeks and

shook her head, her eyes bulging slightly. She leaned closer and closer until I could feel her moist breath on my neck.

"Are those straight pins?" she asked, fighting to keep her voice under control.

"I can explain."

"Who did that to you?" She grabbed my arm. I have never seen Mother so upset before, at least not since the time my cat Stanley ate Donovan's gerbil under the dining room table.

"I did."

"You did?"

"Myself. You know how you are always telling me to think for myself," I reminded her.

She licked her lips. "Didn't it hurt?"

"No," I lied.

"You could have gotten hepatitis."

"What's that?"

"It's a disease." She licked her lips again, not taking her eyes off my ears. "Drug addicts get it from dirty needles."

A cold shiver ran through me. I wasn't worried about myself, but I thought of all the girls I had punched and wondered if any of them would get hepatitis. Maybe that was what was wrong with Sharon. Maybe that was why her ear was red and swollen.

"Is it fatal?"

"Sometimes."

I closed my eyes. I was doomed.

When I opened my eyes again, Mom was still staring at me, her face pale.

"It's not as if I'm going to die or anything," I said. Right then I decided to give her the weekend before I told her the full truth about me. Give the woman a few more days of peace and joy before she had to visit her daughter in jail. Besides, at that moment Donovan came home.

"What are you guys doing?" he asked while he ran a cursory check on the contents of the refrigerator and the cupboards.

"Stacey pierced her ears," said Mother in flat tones.

"Hunh?"

"With straight pins."

"For sure?" For the first time in his life, he looked at me with something akin to admiration.

"I have a note from the principal," I said, trying to change the subject.

Mom read the note, but the subject wasn't changed at all. First she made me take the pins out of my ears, and then she doused them with rubbing alcohol. An icy cold stream of it ran down inside my left ear, where I couldn't even dry it with a cotton swab.

She waited at the door for my father and pounced on him as soon as he came home, before I had a chance to say a single word in self-defense.

Like Jill Williams, Dad didn't think it was the end of the world. He examined my ears and gave me a half-smile. He seemed a lot more interested in the note from Mr. Meeker than in the fact I had put two extra holes in my head.

"What's this with the principal?" he asked.

"Stacey's getting kicked out of school," said Donovan.

I stuck my tongue out at him.

"It's about the award for her paper on Service to Others," said Mom. Boy, was she ever in for a surprise.

"You might put it that way," I said.

"Will Miss Jordan be in the program?" asked Mother. She was a lot happier now that she was thinking of Stacey the Star.

"I don't know. I guess so." At this point, I didn't know if there would be a program. I didn't think elementary schools held court-martial trials in public.

"That poor woman," said Mom.

"Miss Jordan? Poor?" I was surprised. "I didn't know she was poor. She dresses fairly well, and she buys a lot of books."

"She is so unattractive."

"Miss Jordan?" I repeated. I couldn't believe we were talking about the same person.

"What does she look like?" asked Donovan. He had fixed himself a peanut butter, lettuce and mayonnaise sandwich and was stuffing it down. He was also getting crumbs all over the carpet, but Mom never notices when *he* gets crumbs on the carpet.

"She's sort of tall and gangly, gawky."

"She's tall and slender like a fashion model," I said in a rush.

"And she has big overlapping teeth and a terrible complexion."

"Which Miss Jordan do you mean?"

"Why, your teacher. How many Miss Jordans are there?"

"She is wonderful," I shrieked. "And," I groped, "she's not poor. She says anyone who gathers knowledge gathers riches, and she has more knowledge than anybody."

Suddenly the whole day, all of Friday, seemed piled in a big black heap on me. It was too much. I turned and ran upstairs to my room.

10

Miss Jordan *is* ugly. Well, maybe not really ugly. She doesn't frighten babies or anything. But no one will ever call her beautiful. I sat in my seat Monday morning and stared at her, wondering if I had noticed it before. I searched my mind and settled on the very first day of school. I guess I realized that day she wasn't pretty, but I had forgotten it.

And the funny thing about it was that as soon as Miss Jordan started talking, I forgot it again. She was discussing the poem we had been interpreting, and her cheeks were flushed with color, and her clear gray eyes were sparkling. I sighed. There are days when I would sell my soul for clear gray eyes.

The class swung into the daily routine, but for once I wasn't with them. I was too nervous and too tired to worry about being left behind. I hadn't slept much the night before. When I did sleep, I had horrible dreams about mothers screaming "Lynch her. Lynch her." My eyes were dry and scratchy, and my tongue seemed large and furry in my mouth. All in all, I felt like a member of a barbarian horde.

Since I wasn't going to learn anything anyway before ten o'clock, I tried to calm myself by thinking about my birthday the day before. It wasn't very festive. Actually the only good thing about the birthday was my present.

It came in a great big box. "The best things come in big packages," said my dad.

"I think you have that mixed up," said Mother. "Open it, Stacey." I was sitting there, depressed, figuring whatever was in that package was not going to improve my life any.

I was wrong. I tore off the paper and opened the box. There was the tiniest little kitten I have ever seen.

It looked up at me and squeaked more than meowed. I reached down and picked it up, holding it to my chest. It was coal black, its fur long and shiny. I could feel fragile bones under fur and skin.

"It isn't Stanley," I said through the lump in my throat.

"No," said Mom, "but it needs a home, someone to love it."

"I can never love another cat," I said. That wasn't true at all; I already loved it. I even loved the tiny claws that were trying desperately to hang on to me, the bright, curious blue gray eyes.

"Even though you don't like him one little bit," said my dad, "I guess you won't let him starve."

I couldn't help it. I looked up and smiled.

"Why don't you name him Steamer," said Donovan.

"Why should I?" What a dumb name.

"Because he came after Stanley. You know, Stanley Steamer, like the antique car."

"Turn green," I told Donovan.

"The kitten's all black," said Dad. "Maybe you could name him Jinx."

I turned my kitten over, checking him out, even looking into his armpits. He was all black all right. He was totally tarry black. I lifted him to my face and buried my nose in his soft warm fur.

"I'm going to call him Lucky," I said. "I need all the luck I can get."

My daydreaming about Lucky was interrupted by a sharp rap on the classroom door. Miss Bell stuck her head in and said, "Miss Jordan, Mr. Meeker would like to see you in his office."

"Couldn't it wait until eleven?"

"He has to see you now." Miss Bell sounded apologetic. "He said to tell you it would only take five minutes."

"All right." She turned to us students. "I am going to give you your break now. Use it wisely."

Mr. Meeker's five minutes stretched into ten, then into twenty. The girls gathered around my desk, while the boys gathered around Pete's. Pete had sneaked something live into school that morning. I think it was either a snake or a frog, but I wasn't going to find out. I had enough problems.

"What's the beauty secret for today?" Jill asked.

"I don't know." I really didn't care.

"You might as well give the book to me," said Sly. "I don't think you'll be in school for a long time, and I might as well have it to read."

I looked at her silently.

"Stacey could take the book home," said Sharon. "It's checked out in her name."

Sly didn't like that. She gave Sharon a very dirty look.

Sharon didn't seem to care. She was watching me, probably trying to decide what if felt like having a mob of angry parents waiting for me in the principal's office.

She looked somewhat different from Friday. Her earlobe had returned to normal size, and it was pink instead of red. Maybe she wasn't going to die of hepatitis.

"I'd hate to be in your shoes," said Bonnie Adriani. She swung her head. She was wearing huge hoop earrings covered with rhinestones. They sparkled as they moved.

"Much you care," snapped Sly. "Your mother isn't going to be there."

"How do you know?" Bonnie fingered her right ear, twisting the post to make sure the lobe didn't grow shut.

"Because my mother said so. When she brought the note in, she asked Mr. Meeker what mothers were coming."

"My note? You are the person who stole my note?" At first I couldn't believe it. "You stole my note, and your mother gave it to the principal."

"She found it when she was snooping in my purse," said Sly.

"You told me the note was lost."

"So I found it."

"You really are Sly." The words popped out of my mouth. "You're a sneaky, sly witch."

"You'd better not say that." The plane of her cheek was tight; the turquoise eyes glittered. "You take that back."

"Sly Sly," I said.

Sharon's little eyes went from one of us to the other. Bonnie backed away, figeting nervously. Jill and Troylene only watched.

"You call me Sylvia," hissed Sly.

"I'll call you anything I want," I said. "You're a pig and I hate you."

"Stacey," interrupted Jill, too late. I might as well have slit my throat on the spot. I had made an enemy of Sly, and that meant the rest of my days in the sixth grade were going to be miserable beyond belief. Everyone was afraid of Sly and her nasty, sneaking ways except for Tucker, and he didn't have anything to lose. I wished I were suspended and didn't ever have to come back.

Like the good fairy coming to grant my wish, Miss Jordan picked that moment to return.

"Get out your language books," she instructed. "Stacey, it is ten o'clock. You had better go to the office."

I nodded. This time when I gathered my books, she didn't stop me. As I walked past her, she touched my arm.

"Courage, Stacey," she said.

11

I had to wait outside Mr. Meeker's office. Mother waited with me, happy in her ignorant bliss, chattering about awards and service to others and how proud she was of me. I did nothing to wreck her mood. I was busy picturing myself as a sort of nonreligious Joan of Arc with a shaved head.

The door swung open, and Miss Bell came out. Mother gave her a sunny smile. Miss Bell looked confused.

Before the door closed, I could see two women. Probably the rest were out of sight. One of the women had to be Troylene's mother because she was black. Troylene is the only black girl in Miss Jordan's class, and I didn't pierce any of the boys' ears.

"I wish I could take you out for lunch after this," gushed Mother. "I'd love to do something special for you, but I suppose you'll have to stay here and eat in the cafeteria according to school regulations."

I could go away by myself and be a witch, I decided. I could wear a long black gown and big gold hoop earrings and learn to cast spells. The first spell I cast would be over Sylvia Marini. She would lose all her black shiny hair and would weigh 1,000 pounds and have pimples.

Mr. Meeker opened the door and peered into the outer office. He was rubbing his hands nervously together.

"Where is everyone?" he asked.

"I don't know," said Miss Bell. "Perhaps the others aren't coming. They might not have considered it worthwhile."

"How many service awards are there?" asked Mom. She sounded sorry for the kids whose mothers didn't consider it worthwhile to show up for the interview with the principal.

"Service awards?" asked Miss Bell.

Mr. Meeker looked blank.

Miss Bell glanced at me, a mixture of understanding and pity in her blue eyes.

"Why isn't Mrs. Marini here?" asked Mr. Meeker. "She is the person who brought the matter to my attention."

"She called and said she couldn't cancel her hair appointment."

"You mean Sylvia Marini is getting a service award

too?" said Mom. "Isn't that nice, two girls from the same class."

I was thinking dark thoughts about Mrs. Marini. She is as sneaky as her daughter Sly.

"I suppose we've waited long enough," said Mr. Meeker. He cleared his throat. "Would you ladies like to come in here with me?"

Mom followed with the lightheartedness of the pure in thought. I wondered how far I could get if I made a run for it. I wasn't good at running. My feet trotted obediently after Mother.

There were only two other women in the principal's office. Troylene's mother was tall and rather skinny. She was sitting with her legs crossed at the ankles. Her ankles were small and neat and bony. They reminded me of a racehorse. I wished I had ankles like that.

The other mother was a little bit round and very fair skinned with blonde curly hair. I had her figured for Bonnie Adriani's mother.

"Mrs. Kendall, Mrs. Patterson, Mrs. Meleasson," said Mr. Meeker. So, she was Sharon's mother. "And this is Stacey."

Mrs. Patterson gave me a casual glance.

Sharon's mother looked at me as if I belonged in some sort of zoo. She clasped her hands tightly together in her lap, but it was still easy to see they were shaking.

I was surprised to see Sharon's mother there. I wouldn't have thought the pierced ear would have made a bit of difference on Sharon. I mean with all that flab to look at, you wouldn't have thought anyone would notice an extra hole.

Mr. Meeker sat down, then stood up again. "I have here a list of names," he said, and he read off the names of all the girls who had been my customers on Thursday.

Mother frowned. My name wasn't on the list, and she thought it was the awards list.

He looked over the paper at Mother. "These are the girls whose ears Stacey pierced in the girls' lavatory on Thursday," he said. "The lavatory near the Media Center."

"She what?"

"Using," he picked up a pushpin, "I believe, one of these."

"Oh, Stacey," said Mom.

"This is a very serious matter," continued Mr. Meeker. "We must decide here what course of action to take."

"I think she should be suspended," interrupted Mrs. Meleasson. "As an example to others."

"Now hold on a minute," said Mom. She can be like a tiger. When her young are threatened, she becomes dangerous.

"I send Sharon off to school every day, and I expect her to return home exactly as she was when she left in the morning."

"Most of us hope our children will return home with a little more in their heads," said Mom.

"Besides holes," snapped Mrs. Meleasson. Her pale face was turning pink.

"Ladies," said Mr. Meeker.

"Your *daughter*," Mrs. Meleasson made that word sound somehow very dirty, "used that filthy instrument to put a hole in my child's left ear. It became infected. By Friday night, she was crying in pain. I took her to the doctor's Saturday morning, and it cost me twenty-five dollars, twenty-five dollars for the visit and shots." Now her voice was shaking too.

"If money is all you care about," began Mom.

"It isn't the money." Mrs. Meleasson kept getting more and more excited. "I don't want my child defaced."

"Is she defaced?"

"You should see her."

Unfortunately Mother had seen Sharon, in the costume of a frog at the PTA pageant. "See her?" she asked. "How could anyone miss her?"

That was the wrong thing to say. Mrs. Meleasson turned bright red. She looked as if her eyes would pop out of her head.

"Ladies!" said Mr. Meeker sharply.

Mom and Mrs. Meleasson glared at each other.

"Do you have anything to add, Mrs. Patterson?" he asked.

Everyone looked at Mrs. Patterson. She looked back, first at Mrs. Meleasson who was breathing hard and was so red that she looked like a possible stroke victim. Then she glanced at Mom, who was also having difficulty breathing, but who had clenched fists and glittering eyes. At last she turned her dark eyes on me.

She began to giggle. Then she laughed right out loud.

"Mrs. Patterson," said Mr. Meeker. It was clear he thought her mind had flipped out from the strain.

"I'm sorry," she said. Then she hiccuped. "But after all, it is funny."

"Funny?" Mrs. Meleasson couldn't believe she heard right.

"All this fuss over some child's tricks." She looked sternly at the principal. "I had forgotten about this meeting. I really came in here to find out why the children aren't allowed to learn about art anymore."

"No one said they couldn't learn about art," said Mr. Meeker in a hurry.

"Troylene tells me you took away Miss Jordan's pictures."

"Yes, well." He blinked rapidly. Obviously he preferred to talk about the sins of Stacey Kendall. "One of the parents complained—"

"You mean because of the sick mind of one individual, you would deprive our children of the right to an education?" Mrs. Patterson looked very formidable and not at all easy to convince.

"Ah." Mr. Meeker was definitely uneasy now. As far as he was concerned, it was all right to discuss student mistakes in front of adults. It was not all right to discuss adult mistakes in the presence of students. "Perhaps Stacey should return to class before we talk about this."

"You're not kicking me out of school?"

"I have not yet reached a decision." He stared at me through the bottom of his glasses. "Of course, suspension is the most likely decision, but I did have a conversation with Miss Jordan, who convinced me that this might not be the appropriate response."

"Oh."

"You will return to class."

So it was back to Sly Sylvia. As I gathered my books from my lap and got to my feet, I felt as if I were being thrown to the lions, or at least to the weasels.

I looked at Mrs. Meleasson before I went out the door. She didn't seem at all angry now, only tired. I glanced at Mom. She was sitting there with her eyes shut. Probably she never wanted to see my face again.

I walked slowly down the hall toward class, my life in shreds. Ignoring the fact that it had been my idea to pierce ears, I concentrated my thoughts on Sylvia Marini. I hoped she got gangrene and her head dropped off. That would teach her.

12

No one said anything to me the rest of the day, not even at lunch. I guess, for the other kids, it was like being around a terminally ill person. You sit around waiting for her to die and can't think of a single thing to say that she might want to hear.

The only good thing about the situation was that Sly left me alone. She was probably gathering her forces and laying plans to take me by surprise. Whatever she did would be no surprise to me. From now on, I was going to be the loneliest kid in the sixth grade.

When I arrived home from school, Mom was lying on the couch, a damp cloth on her forehead, her eyes closed. There was an open aspirin bottle on the coffee table. At first I thought she had overdosed on aspirin, but then she slowly opened her eyes and stared at me.

"You mutilated seven people," she said.

Actually it was seven and one half. She had forgotten about Sharon.

I tried a sort of dumb but friendly smile. It didn't work.

At that moment, Donovan arrived. He always chooses the most critical times of my life to butt in. He glanced at Mom on the sofa, went to the kitchen and made himself a cheese sandwich, and came back into the living room gnawing on it. His appetite is disgusting.

"Is she sick?" he asked. Mom had her eyes closed again. Either her head really hurt or she was putting on a good act.

"I think she has a headache."

"Who's going to cook dinner?"

"There might not be any dinner," said Mom, sitting up and snatching the cloth off her forehead. "Stacey, what are you doing there with your coat on?"

"I was thinking of running away."

"No dinner?" Donovan's world fell apart. He squinted at Mom, chewing convulsively. "Did something happen to Dad?"

"Of course not." She waved a hand at me. "Maybe you ought to ask your sister."

Donovan looked at me. I stuck out my tongue. It is one of my favorite forms of communication with him.

"What did she do?" he asked.

"She pierced the ears of seven girls. In the lavatory." Mom spaced her words evenly. "Near the Media Center. Thursday."

"For sure?" His eyes lit up.

"Seven and one half girls," I corrected modestly. At least somebody appreciated my efforts.

"I'm glad you think it's funny." Mom's voice rose, a little bit like when she had the fight with Mrs. Meleasson, only now she sounded more upset than angry. "When I think of all the hours and days and weeks, years, that I have tried to teach you—"

I had never thought of my mother as the hysterical type. Crisis situations do strange things to people. I put my coat and books away and went to the kitchen and turned the oven to 350 degrees in case she felt like cooking anything. Then I got Lucky out of his box and fed him a little warmed milk.

He wasn't interested in warmed milk. He was more interested in crawling all over me and mewing.

"You didn't bring me much luck yet," I whispered softly to him. It wasn't his fault. He was only a beginner at being lucky, and I had a pretty big problem for him to work on.

Donovan came to the kitchen and started pulling TV dinners out of the freezer, peeling them and shoving them in the oven.

"She okay in there?" I asked.

"Probably." He shrugged his shoulders. "I think she's pretending to sleep so she doesn't have to look at us."

I took a piece of string out of a drawer and began to

play on the floor with Lucky. He pranced across the blue and white tile, batting at the string. I told myself I would remember him like this forever.

"You think they'll suspend you?"

"I don't know."

"Nobody in our family was ever suspended before."

"There's always a first time for everything." I thought of the scene in the principal's office and shuddered.

My kitten did bring me a little luck. Whether it was from all the aspirin or from emotional exhaustion, Mom did fall asleep on the couch. When Dad came home, he looked down at her and then very quietly came into the kitchen.

"What's the matter with your mother?" he asked.

I bent my head, watching Lucky play between my legs, waiting for Donovan's traitorous answer.

"I think she has a headache," he said.

"I'm sorry I stuck my tongue out at you," I told him. He isn't rotten clear through the way Sly is.

"That's okay." He shrugged. Avoiding Dad's eyes, he watched the TV dinners through the window in the oven door.

"Is there some sort of problem?"

Neither of us answered.

"Is everything all right at school?"

"Everything's all wrong," I said. He had to know sometime. "I never want to go back there. I don't even want to go back tomorrow. Do I have to?"

"Of course you have to. It's the law."

"I could go to Catholic school." I had not thought of

Catholic school before, but suddenly it seemed like my only chance.

"We're Methodist."

"Well, why don't Methodists have special schools?"

"You aren't being logical," said Dad.

"Besides," I added. "I'm sure Saint Joe's would take me. I've heard they're desperate for warm bodies." I was warm all right. I was so warm I was drenched with sweat.

"Stacey." Dad got down on his haunches to look me in the eyes, the way he used to when I was a little kid. "What is the matter? Come on. Tell me about it."

"The trouble is that she mutilated seven other children," said my mother in flat tones from the doorway. She had awakened and come to the kitchen. Her hair was all mussed up from sleeping, and she was very pale.

"She what?" Dad stood up abruptly.

"She pierced holes in the ears of seven other girls."

There was a long second of quiet.

My dad and Mrs. Patterson have a lot in common. They both have a sense of humor. He struggled to control himself and then burst out laughing.

"Why does everyone think this is funny?" said Mom, her voice full of outrage. She stared at Donovan.

"I didn't do nothing," he protested. "I just put the TV dinners in the oven."

Dad was still laughing. He gradually slowed and stopped as Mom glared at him.

"Are you finished now?" she asked coldly.

"Yes."

"Then perhaps you can help me decide what we are going to do about this child."

Dad looked down at me. I picked Lucky off the floor and put him back in his box where he would be safe in case anything bad happened. My hands were shaking like Mrs. Meleasson's.

"I think we ought to buy her earrings," said Dad.

Put me up against Mr. Meeker and hordes of angry mothers and I remain unshaken, on the outside anyway. But a few kind words can bring me to tears. I dropped my face in my hands and started crying.

13

Pariah was our word for the day. A pariah is an outcast, one who is despised by society. Somehow it seemed suitable. Miss Jordan must have chosen it with me in mind.

I knew first thing in the morning that the kids were going to ignore me the way they had the day before. The only exception was Tucker. He stopped by my desk on the way to his own seat.

"Nice going, kid," he said, punching me hard on my left arm. For Tucker, a friendly punch is a high compliment. My arm hurt all morning, but I was grateful. There is nothing like a little physical pain to take one's mind off other problems.

Sly gathered most of the girls into a corner near the chalkboard. They looked like a bouquet of flowers in their different colored tops and jeans as they were whispering together. I couldn't help but notice that practically all of them wore earrings. Bonnie had on the big rhinestone hoops that she had worn Monday. Jill had her little gold daisy studs. She and Sharon kept looking at me when Sly wasn't watching.

Troylene hurried into the room one minute before the bell rang. She had big gold hoops in her ears. They looked absolutely beautiful with her big Afro. She glanced at me, shook her head, and rushed to her seat.

Sly wasn't in any hurry. She stopped at my desk the way Tucker had, but she didn't punch me in the arm. She leaned over, her eyes dangerous. "My dad is going to sue your parents," she whispered. "You're going to lose your house and all your money."

Sylvia always knows the perfect way to cheer someone up. I bowed my head over my paper and stayed that way all through language. I didn't even raise it when Miss Jordan called on me. Miss Jordan hates that; she calls it mumble-mouthing.

At eleven, Miss Jordan called break. I stayed in my seat, waiting for the girls to gather again in the corner by the chalkboard, waiting for just one of them to have pity and stop by my desk to find out the beauty hint of the day.

Jill and Troylene might have. They were definitely headed my direction when Sly put her hands on their arms. She talked low and fast, gesturing toward a small package that lay on her desk. When she picked up the package, Jill and Troylene went with the others. Jill gave me an apologetic shrug. It probably indicated some sort of pity for the untouchable.

For one wild moment I considered following the girls to the lavatory. Then logical thinking took over. If I followed them, Sly was sure to come up with something like splashing me with toilet water. Instead, I read *1,001 Ways To Be Beautiful.*

"Always have a sunny disposition," the book instructed. "Everyone loves a smiling face."

I pulled my lips back over my teeth in a ghastly grin. I held it that way until I felt like a fool. My ears itched, and I couldn't scratch them. I didn't know if they itched because the girls were talking about me in the lavatory or because they were healing. Either way it was very annoying.

"Hey." Pete Parsons stopped by my desk. "Why aren't you out with the other girls?"

"Because I'm not crazy, that's why."

"They're the ones who are crazy," said Pete. "Marini stinks. Want me to tell her to shut up about you?"

"No, thanks."

It was hot in the room. Pete's red hair seemed like a bonfire on top of his freckled face. He patted the ball between his hands, back and forth, back and forth.

"I could lie in wait for her at the bus stop. No one

would ever know." His brown eyes sparkled at the thought of getting at Sly.

"It's okay. Really it is," I lied.

"Peter, Peter, pumpkin eater," shouted Stevie.

"Had a girl and couldn't keep her," finished Tucker.

Pete's face suddenly matched his hair. He started chasing Tucker, who chased Stevie. Somehow when Miss Jordan and the girls came back into the room, Stevie was seated at his desk reading a book and Pete and Tucker were acting like a barbarian horde. Miss Jordan didn't say a word to either one of them, but she gave Stevie a sharp look. Miss Jordan is nobody's fool.

In the cafeteria, my table was empty. Usually Bonnie and Sly and Missy and Pam and Sharon are there with me, but the first four crowded in with Jill, and Sharon was still in line buying extra milk. I sat at the bare expanse of table and acted as if I were enjoying my lunch.

Mrs. Withers walked by. She hardly looked at me. I reflected bitterly that the other girls weren't allowed to move their seats in the middle of the school year. If Miss Jordan had had cafeteria duty or Mrs. Knopf or practically anybody else, they would have made the girls return to their original tables. Mrs. Withers only looked from the crowded table to my empty one and gave a little smile. She was probably happy to see someone in trouble besides her.

While I pretended to be eating my mystery sandwich, Sharon came chugging up with her tray. She stood for a moment, bewilderment on her fat features. Then she looked towards Jill's table. There was no way she could push in.

When she slapped her tray down across from me, some of the chocolate milk splashed out of her open carton, but she didn't seem to notice. She sat down and began stuffing herself.

"Didn't you make some sort of mistake?" I asked.

"Hunh?" She looked up at me, pushing a stray piece of lettuce into her mouth with her little finger.

"Don't you have the wrong table?" I felt so miserable that the words came out sneering and nasty.

Sharon is used to people being ugly toward her. "I always sit here," she said.

"What if your mother finds out? I'm not exactly her most favorite person."

"Listen." Sharon stopped chewing and swallowed. "You'll have to ignore my mother. She is under a great strain. It's not easy to be the mother of a fat kid."

"What?" I was so surprised I forgot to sound nasty.

"Try to look at life from her point of view. There is enough of me to be twins, but there is no way she can trade me in on a set. She has to go around pretending that she doesn't care that I'm fat, that the kid waiting in line for seconds isn't her daughter, and that she doesn't mind when she has to order me special clothes from a catalog. I think she cries a lot."

It was a long speech for Sharon. She began eating again. It occurred to me that Sharon never had much

83

of a chance to say anything in our group of girls. It also occurred to me that I had never really paid much attention to Sharon, except for her flab. I looked at her closely.

Those folds around Sharon's eyes were smile lines. I looked more closely. I had never noticed, but her eyes were a deep periwinkle blue.

"You have beautiful eyes," I blurted.

"Not that again!" Sharon slapped herself on the forehead. "Every stinking time my mother wants to get me on a diet, she lists my attractive points. So far the only one she has found is my eyes."

"Don't you want to be beautiful?"

"Sometimes." She shrugged. "But not enough to give up food. Besides—"

"Besides what?"

"I figure if I get down to normal human-being size, then I'll just have a lot of other hassles, like boys and dates and all that yuk."

"That's not yuk!"

"Yes, it is."

"You're running away from hassles," I said. "You're scared!"

Sharon didn't care.

"Right," she admitted. "Also, I love food. I even love mystery sandwiches." She looked at mine.

"You want it? I'm not very hungry."

"I thought you'd never ask." She scooped it up.

I laughed. Suddenly I could understand Sharon. Suddenly I even liked her. "I'm sorry I only pierced one of your ears," I said.

"That's okay. If you'd pierced both, I would have had two infections." The blue eyes studied me.

"Could you come over to my house Saturday afternoon?" she asked, so quietly that I could barely hear her.

"Your mother would kill me."

"No she won't. If she tries anything violent, I'll sit on her and mash her flat."

"Okay," I agreed.

It's funny, but until that moment I had never seen Sharon smile. Oh, I'd seen cautious little half-smiles, but this was a big open, honest grin. It transformed her whole face. The lines around her eyes really were smile lines. Her periwinkle eyes shone.

Mom says that beauty is only skin-deep. Maybe with Sharon, you have to go a few extra layers. She grabbed up her tray and left the table before I could change my mind about going to her house.

Across the cafeteria tables I saw Sly staring at me, her eyes slitted. Her tongue flicked out and back like a snake's. With a sinking feeling, I realized that by joining up with Sharon I really had become a pariah, a social outcast.

Think positive, I told myself. I like Sharon better than Sly anyway. I picked up my milk and took a long, refreshing drink.

14

Early the next morning, Mr. Meeker called Miss Jordan to his office again. Miss Bell stayed with us until Miss Jordan came back. She didn't relax for a second. She stood at the front of the room, her shoulders stiff and her eyes darting from one student to another. Mostly they darted at Tucker.

Since I was working on my interpretation of "Pied Beauty," I read the poem five times. The first four times it didn't make any sense at all. Then it occurred to me that Hopkins was writing to thank God about different kinds of beauty. The poem was still very difficult, especially those lines about "All things counter, original, spare, strange; Whatever is fickle, freckled . . ."

I thought about those lines a lot. The same as artists, poets must have different ideas from the rest of us of what is beautiful. The poet wasn't writing about fat women though. He was writing about fickle and freckled. He could have been writing about Pete Parsons. Pete is freckled all right.

It was fun thinking that the poem could have been about Pete. I amused myself for several minutes trying to list all the ways the lines could have referred to him. As a result, I did hardly any work at all.

Miss Jordan came back looking very harassed, but rather triumphant. Maybe she had tied Mr. Meeker up and thrown him into a corner of his office, so he couldn't interrupt her teaching anymore.

She thanked Miss Bell and got her out of the room. Then she turned toward the class. I bent my head over my desk, preparing to mumble-mouth.

Miss Jordan hates it when students won't participate. She picks on them right away. This time she didn't hesitate for a second.

"Stacey," she said. "What is Hopkins writing about in 'Pied Beauty'?"

"Pete Parsons," I said.

There was total silence. Total silence was followed by gales of laughter. Tucker fell out of his seat and rolled on the floor, clutching at his stomach and wheezing. Sharon laughed right out loud. Miss Jordan laughed. Even Pete laughed.

In a pause during which everyone tried to catch their breath, Troylene said, "Miss Jordan. Miss Jordan. I don't understand."

That set everyone off again.

Finally Miss Jordan got us back in order. She wiped the tears from her eyes and smiled at me. "Stacey," she said. "Sometimes I think you don't know how grateful I am to have you in this class."

Every class needs a jester, I thought sourly, someone to laugh at. For my next trick, I will learn to balance balls on the end of my nose.

"Unfortunately we are going to have to do without you for a little while at least. You are to report to Mr. Meeker's office."

How long was a little while? Five minutes or five years? It made no difference to me, I tried to tell myself as I trudged down the hall.

Mr. Meeker's office had been seen so much by me in the past week that it was becoming very familiar territory. Even the chair I sat in was familiar. A few more visits and I expected to find a brass plaque on the back saying: RESERVED FOR STACEY KENDALL.

Mr. Meeker didn't look as worried as he had on Monday. Either he had finally settled on my punishment or he had started taking tranquilizers. I hoped he had decided on my punishment. I figured a few more days of suspense, and I would crack under the strain. If I didn't, Mom definitely would. She's been going around hollow-eyed since Monday. Every once in a while I catch her staring at me, a strange expression on her face. When I catch her, she pretends she is looking at something else, but she is staring at me all right.

"Well, Stacey," he said. For once he didn't rub his hands together.

I didn't say anything. I mean, how do you answer something like that?

"Miss Jordan came in to see me this morning."

That wasn't exactly true. Actually he had sent for Miss Jordan, but far be it from me to point out any of Mr. Meeker's mistakes.

"We discussed your little problem with seven other girls."

Seven and a half. And I am glad he considers it a little problem.

"She doesn't think you should be suspended."

"Every class needs a clown."

His mouth dropped open. "You said something?"

"No, sir."

He looked very suspicious. There were only two of us in the room, and someone had said something. Finally he continued.

"Miss Jordan says you have a fine record and that she would hate to see you miss any school. She also says she is certain the incident was the result of an innocent mistake."

I waited.

"With this in mind, I called Mrs. Meleasson. She agreed that perhaps the situation is not as serious as we first thought."

"What about Mrs. Martini?" I interrupted.

"Who?"

"Mrs. Marini," I corrected.

"Er, she was unavailable for comment."

"Oh."

"Therefore, you will write a paper on what you have learned from the events of the past few weeks. You will present this paper at the awards assembly Friday."

"Hunh?"

"I think at this time it would be a little indelicate for you to present your paper on Service to Others, although you will receive your award. You earned that. Since your name is already on the program, I think it is fair that you make some sort of presentation to the student body. A speech concerning your recent mistakes will be acceptable."

Terrific. I had to stand up in front of the entire school and tell them I made a fool of myself. My mind worked quickly. Perhaps I could come up with some sort of speech that would get me off the hook with Mr. Meeker and get back at Sly at the same time.

"And Stacey."

"Yes."

"I want a copy of that speech on my desk the morning before you present it."

So much for that idea. I left the office, my mood only a little improved by the fact that I had not been suspended. I almost think I would rather have been suspended than write another paper. My fingers were practically worn out from writing papers.

My mood wasn't improved when I noticed during lunch that Sly had a new set of gold hoops in her ears.

The quest for beauty had led us down some strange paths. Everyone had gained something from it. Sharon might have had an infected ear, but at least she was smiling. Troylene was more terrific looking than ever, and Bonnie seemed happy with her rhinestones. What did Sly get out of it? Gold earrings. What did I get? Heartache. Heartache and a paper to write. Sometimes life just isn't fair.

15

When Mom tells me to do something I really don't want to do, like write thank-you notes for my birthday presents, I usually postpone it by cleaning my room. I would have cleaned my room from top to bottom before I wrote my paper for Mr. Meeker, but I didn't have time to mess around like that. After school, I collected Lucky from his box and took him upstairs with me. In my room I could concentrate, without Mom staring at me.

I moved the lamp from my dresser to my desk, threw a pile of comic books and magazines and old pieces of paper from my desk onto the floor, and sat down to think.

First I organized my thoughts on paper, the way Miss Jordan had taught us. I wrote a list of what I had learned.

1. Miss Jordan is ugly but a great teacher.
2. My mother is a hysteric.
3. My father is a warm and understanding human being.
4. Sylvia Marini is pretty, but rotten clear through.
5. Jill Williams is nice although she is pretty.
6. Sharon is a real person under all that fat.
7. If I ever pierce any more ears, I will make sure I sterilize the pin every time.

As I studied the list and made some additions, I munched some stale Cheese Puffs that were hidden in my top dresser drawer. They are very nourishing and low in calories. I fed two to Lucky who was sitting on my lap.

The Cheese Puffs gave Lucky lots of energy. He dug his little claws into my red top and climbed the whole way up it to where he could jump onto the top of my desk. He batted at my pencil with one little paw and then chased the point around as I wrote. When I stopped writing to think about my list, he tried to move the tip of the pencil himself.

Then he threw up on the paper.

He is lucky all right. He is lucky I didn't kill him.

I carefully folded the paper and put it into my waste basket. Then I moved Lucky to my bed where he couldn't chase my pencil anymore. He gave a little cough as if he might throw up again; so I picked him off my bed and took him to Donovan's room, where I shut him in the closet. When I went back downstairs, I could free him.

When I had made a new list and had it properly organized, I wrote my paper. In the process, I made some more additions and left some parts out. I left out the part about my parents as I didn't think the student body would be interested. I added something about Mr. Meeker. They are always interested in Mr. Meeker. Then I took my speech and went downstairs.

Mom was sitting in the living room on the couch in front of the window. She had her legs tucked up under her, and her eyes had the same glazed appearance they had on Monday. At least she wasn't at the aspirin bottle again.

"Is everything all right?" I asked.

"Sure." She didn't sound convinced.

"You look worried."

"I'm worried about all the work you are going to miss when you are suspended from school."

"I'm not going to be suspended. I'm even going to get my award for Service to Others. The only punishment Mr. Meeker gave me was to write a speech and give it in assembly tomorrow on what I learned from my mistakes."

I don't think she believed me at first, but when I asked for her and Dad to listen to my speech she cheered up.

"Your father's at his bowling league dinner," she

said, "but I'll be glad to listen." She uncurled her legs and bounced on the couch like a little kid. It is amazing how fast my mom can recover from life's little tragedies.

I stood in the middle of the room, my feet together, my paper held in front of me. I tried to pretend that there were 300 students and all of the teachers at Medford Elementary facing me, instead of only Mom. I cleared my throat.

"Good morning," I read. "I want to tell you what an honor it is to be here." I didn't say a pleasure, because it definitely wasn't a pleasure. Then I said some garbage about being sorry for my crimes and what a great school we had, and then I got to the important part about what I had learned from the events of the past week.

"I learned that beauty is more than skin-deep," I said. "But there is no sense piercing holes in yourself or others trying to find it. Give it a chance, and it will come out by itself. In some people, beauty is a shy little animal who tries to hide."

Mom smiled.

"I mean, take someone like Sharon Meleasson." I continued. "She might be fat on the outside, but inside there is a terrific kid with a great sense of humor."

Mom choked. I sped on.

"Look at Miss Jordan. No one in their right mind would ever call her beautiful, but she is a super person and the world's greatest teacher.

Mom winced. "Maybe you could phrase that a little differently," she said.

"Please don't interrupt," I said. "I'll lose my place if you interrupt."

I ran my eyes down over my paper, found my place, and continued as if Mom hadn't said anything.

"I learned that Sylvia Marini might have a pretty face and shiny long hair, but she is a big rat just like her mother." I chuckled inside. Mr. Meeker wouldn't like that. He would be afraid of trouble with Mrs. Marini.

Thinking about Mr. Meeker led me into the next part.

"I learned that Mr. Meeker doesn't have a real understanding of what an education is all about. He took away Miss Jordan's art reproductions and locked them in his safe because some parent couldn't understand them, but he made a great big fuss over what was really only a silly little mistake."

I paused.

Mom was squirming around on the couch as if she were having some sort of fit or had to go to the bathroom. She doesn't like it when I squirm on the couch. She says it is hard on the material, but there she was, squirming away.

"What do you think?" I asked.

"I think your presentation needs a little more work."

"I'm not finished yet." My mom is so pessimistic. She should learn to think positive like my dad. I turned the page over and skipped the part about Jill Williams, since Jill is basically shy and probably wouldn't like me to talk about her in assembly. I skipped to the end of my speech.

"Therefore, because of the influence of Mr. Meeker and my sincere desire to apologize to everyone for causing trouble, I am making this speech," I said. I paused dramatically. "I apologize for the sins of Stacey Kendall," I finished grandly.

"I like that last part," said Mom.

"Thank you."

"But I think that you are going to have to change some of the rest of it."

"But Mother, I worked two hours on this speech," I howled. She doesn't like it when I criticize her articles on the financial pages.

"Hey! Did you want me to listen for my help in making it better, or did you only want me to say you are wonderful?"

"Okay." I sighed. "What's wrong with it?"

She started to tell me, but Donovan interrupted, the way he always does. He can't stand to see me get one little bit of attention. He came running downstairs and into the living room.

"Mom," he yelled. "The cat threw up in my good shoes!"

16

Medford Elementary always holds its awards day for scholastic achievement in April. That is because the big school talent show is in May, and the last assembly of the year, in June, is kept for the awards in sports and in attendance. Besides giving out prizes for good grades and helping in the Media Center, the special award for the best paper on Service to Others is given in the scholastic assembly. My paper took first place this year. Jill Williams' paper took second. There was no third place.

Since I was being punished and couldn't read my paper, Jill had to read hers. As I have mentioned, Jill is basically shy, so she was very nervous. She turned pale, held on to the lectern for support, and read in such a low voice that only the kids who were on the stage and the people in the front row could hear her. That was all right. Her paper wasn't very exciting. All she did was list the different definitions of *service* and then tell how she tried to fulfill each one. My paper was a lot better. No wonder it took first place. But I didn't get to read it. Instead, I had to give my apologizing speech.

Actually my speech wasn't much different from the one I had read to Mom the night before. Mostly it was a matter of changing the wording and leaving some things out. For instance, I told them about Miss Jordan's being a super person and the world's greatest teacher, but I didn't mention the fact she isn't beautiful. I said Sharon has a great sense of humor and did not refer at all to her flab. I left the part about Sly and her mother out entirely, although I did take a passing swipe at Mr. Meeker for taking Miss Jordan's art reproductions.

My mother did something very admirable that day. She showed up for the assembly. Now a lot of mothers would show up for an assembly during which their kid gets some sort of prize handed to them. My mother is the only mother I know who would come to hear her kid apologize in front of the entire school. For that matter, she is the only mother I know who has ever actually had the opportunity to hear her kid apologize in front of the whole school.

My speech was a great success. The students

stamped their feet and whistled and cheered. Tucker shook his hands over his head, fists together, in a victory sign. Actually, I think a lot of the students were whistling and cheering because my speech marked the end of the assembly and it was almost time for lunch, but I pretended all the applause was for me. I bowed graciously and said, "Thank you."

"Mr. Meeker wants me in his office," whispered Jill, as we stood on the stage watching the students clear the assembly.

"What did you do?" I stared at Jill. She didn't look guilty of anything.

"Nothing. He said he wants me to carry a pile of stuff back to Miss Jordan's room. He said I should get someone to help me. Will you?"

"Go with you to the principal's office?"

"Yes."

"My feet could find it in the dark."

"We're to wait here until the halls are empty."

As we waited for the last of the kindergartners to straggle out of the room, I studied Jill. How I envied her clear complexion tinged with pink over the cheekbones, her delicate figure, her small hands and feet. I felt so big and horsey beside her, awkward and disgustingly healthy-looking.

"What are you staring at?"

"You. You're so lucky. I wish I looked like you," I mourned.

"Like me?" Jill's brown eyes widened with astonishment. "Stacey Kendall, you are the lucky one."

"Sure. I get into big trouble and have to apologize to the whole school."

"Anyone else would have been suspended. Anyone else would never have gotten away with piercing everybody's ears and then crossing Sylvia Marini. You can do anything you want." She thought for a second and then continued in hushed tones. "You can even go over to Sharon's if you want to." She made going over to Sharon's sound like the most terrific social event of the year.

"You can too, if you really want to," I pointed out. "Come on. Everyone's back in class except for us." We walked slowly down the empty hall toward the office. A long ray of light made the dust show up on the tile floor, made the grubby fingerprints on the windows by the gym emerge in every smudgy detail. With a sudden attack of sorrow, I realized that after two more months I would never walk these halls again.

"You're so lucky," continued Jill, not noticing the dust and the fingerprints. "Everybody likes you."

"Me?" I squeaked. Surely she didn't mean Stacey Kendall, girl pariah.

"You're popular and smart and funny all at the same time. No one else would ever say that 'Pied Beauty' was about Pete Parsons. No one else would ever think it."

We were at the office, so I didn't have time to think about what Jill had said. I tucked it away in one corner of my mind for later.

Mr. Meeker didn't seem overjoyed to see me. He

didn't even offer me my usual chair. He just had Jill and me hold out our arms while he loaded them with piles of posters. The posters were rolled with the pictures inside, so we couldn't see them. It was hard to balance them and to walk at the same time.

Miss Jordan must have been expecting us. She held the door open, then ushered us to the back of the room, where she has a long table she keeps for projects. She took the posters from our arms and stacked them neatly on the end of the table that was against the wall.

When she resumed her place at the front of the room, there was the tiniest hint of triumph in her clear gray eyes. All those rolled up posters were her art reproductions, liberated from Mr. Meeker's safe.

17

Between Friday and Monday I had a lot of time to think. Besides going to Sharon's Saturday afternoon, I did little else besides think and play with my kitten.

I thought a lot about all the fun I had with Sharon on Saturday. We let her guinea pig loose and chased it around the house until it squeezed into the cold air intake to the furnace and disappeared.

Mrs. Meleasson became hysterical. She said the guinea pig would get into the furnace and fry and that the whole house would stink for months. I suggested putting a cat into the cold air intake to catch the guinea pig, but she only glared at me balefully through red-rimmed eyes. At that point, Sharon suggested what she called a munch break for hot fudge sundaes sprinkled with peanuts.

Besides thinking about Saturday at Sharon's, I thought about what Jill had said about my being popular. I decided that at age almost twelve, really age eleven, I had been a mere infant, placing emphasis on things that aren't important, such as physical attractiveness. Now I am much more mature, going on thirteen, practically a teenager. I know that what is most important in my life is my relationships with other people.

Jill says I am popular. Mom says I'm notorious, which is something entirely different. *Notorious* means famous in a bad sort of way. Anyway, I am well known. As a matter of fact, I am probably the best-known sixth grader in all of Medford School.

That is all right. Since I'm no great beauty and I haven't got a giant brain, I have decided that by the time I reach age thirteen, I will become wildly popular. The only problem is getting the other kids to agree. I am working on it.

This morning before school I checked a book out of the Media Center. It is called *1,001 Ways To Be Popular*. I only had time to shove the book into my desk when Miss Jordan began class.

"I have a fine new project, or rather an old one, for you people," she said, excitement dancing in her voice and eyes alike. "For it, I want you to separate into groups of five, one project and one group a week."

"Stacey is going to head the first division," she continued. "Who will help her?"

"I will," said Sharon.

"Oh, bleep," said Sly.

Let's face it. With Sharon and me in the same group, Miss Jordan was never going to get another volunteer.

"I will," offered Jill.

"Figures," said Sly.

"Me too," said Troylene.

This time Sly kept her mouth shut. We were beginning to look like a crowd.

"Me too," echoed a small voice from the back of the room. It was Joy Davis, a little girl who is quiet as a mouse. This is the first time all year that she has volunteered for anything.

"You can come to my house tomorrow after school," said Sharon. "I'll bake a cheesecake tonight."

Already I could feel my trouble spots multiplying.

"I'll bring some diet pop," offered Jill. The whole thing was beginning to sound like a party.

"Aren't you girls interested in what the project is?" asked Miss Jordan. She unrolled one of her posters. It was a reproduction of a big still life painting in bright colors with some pottery and some fruit on a pale tablecloth. "Paul Cézanne," she said. *Still Life With Apples.*"

"I like the ones with fat ladies better," said Tucker.

"Now," continued Miss Jordan after she had pinned the reproduction to the bulletin board, "our poem of the week. It's by William Shakespeare, 'Full Fathom Five,' something different from what you have been accustomed to."

I settled back happily to listen. Life was back to normal.